A Unison of Breaths

Lynda Tavakoli

A UNISON OF BREATHS

ARLEN
HOUSE

A Unison of Breaths

is published in 2024 by
ARLEN HOUSE
42 Grange Abbey Road
Baldoyle
Dublin D13 A0F3
Ireland
Email: arlenhouse@gmail.com
www.arlenhouse.ie

ISBN 978–1–85132–332–6, paperback

International distribution
SYRACUSE UNIVERSITY PRESS
621 Skytop Road, Suite 110
Syracuse
New York 13244–5290
USA
Email: supress@syr.edu
www.syracuseuniversitypress.syr.edu

Typesetting by Arlen House

Cover image by Emma Barone

CONTENTS

for my sister, Jean,
the kindest person I know.

A Unison of Breaths

HARRY DIED TODAY
for Maude

On the page,
in my mother's
fading hand,
a date,
scorched into a calendar's
stark month.

Three small words,
spilling their truth
like spindrift,
and blown across
the surface of her
empty sea.

Cold Tea

In the good room of our small bungalow
mum read tea leaves from china cups
rescued from the Oxfam shop,
her slight frame and unassuming manner
a mere subterfuge for her divining skills.

There were rules – never on a Sunday
and never in the company of my aunt.
I don't expect our dad much approved either
but he let it go, understanding that some things
are probably best left undisturbed.

Believers came to swallow readings
with the trust of any never on the Sabbath
congregation and sculpted dregs of faith
round porcelain curves. Prophesies of doom
were subtly laid aside for Sunday sermons.

I sometimes wonder if she'd seen her future
buried in the leaves. An arrow (never good news),
snakes (the same), or wavy lines portending
journeys unfulfilled. But if she did, it was for none
of us to know, for that was not our mother's way.

Looking back, I should have read the signs myself –
cups of tea, half drunk and cold, perched
on the bird table or teetering on bathroom shelves
and once or twice abandoned by our father's garden tools,
that sedge of herons she had planted by the pond.

It's the way I like to drink it, she would say, the dare
in her eyes always enough, and later,

tea leaves carefully strained, I would present to her
a sun, a fish, a flying bird and catch her smile,
cupped in her hands the white lie of a daughter's love.

POUFFE

After she died and we were clearing her things,
I kept the better looking, shop-bought one.
The pouffe with the pizzazz of oh la la
and home for weary feet to fantasise
a cancan on The Avenue des Champs-Élysées.
I gave the other one away.

She had made that one herself.
Six National Dried Milk tins
saved from the war, covered
and re-covered from the burden
of my father's bog-trodden,
hard-soled, Fermanagh feet.

And the final reincarnation
created from a benefactor's castoffs;
a coat, as hirsute as any camel,
its buttons big as biscuits
that we bought together
from some charity sale in Fivemiletown.

Sometimes it's just too late;
hearts forever squeezed
by the sharpness of a memory
of what we gave away in haste.
Those small, important things, laid bare
with the ever-present cruelty of hindsight.

A VILLAGE PRACTICE

I find him attractive in that young and self-assured
dentist kind of way and I imagine, in my earlier life,
there could have been a spark of something there.
My mother waits in his chair, her brittle mouth only small.
I am told to sit in the corner and I do, examining
the cleanliness of the room, pondering how it cloys
in the disinfectant spaces between us.

He prises apart her poor jaw, chooses a drill.
The stickered soles of my mother's shoes twitch
with some invisible electric shock
but the rest of her is numb, except her mouth,
which is not. I am her voice and the palliative
care of her crumbling teeth, yet I am reticent.
It does not do to question authority, regardless of age.

And pain relief, I ask. The request an unforeseen
tsunami across the room, a sudden game of Truth or Dare.
She doesn't need it. She does. She doesn't.
I cannot see my mother's eyes but imagine them sealed,
blanking out the embarrassment of my irreverence
in this community where people talk. *She does.*
And his slender fingers finally find a syringe.

In the waiting room muted exchanges churn
around the lateness of the milking, or how
the silage has seen two cuts already the year.
We shuffle home, wordless. I want her to be proud of me
for standing up for her but worry that I went too far.
So she makes the tea, her bent shoulders stiff
in concentration. *Good girl,* she says. *Good girl.*

DAY ROOM DAYS

This morning the shell of you
waits in the day room,
a shrinking form more
tortoise-like than yesterday.
Nipped between finger and thumb,
a biscuit, the warm chocolate
already sculpting patterns
into your grooved palm.

Hibernating eyes shift.
What's this for you say,
not even a question,
and there are no words
except perhaps the ones I should
have said before they wouldn't matter.
Now they rain as shadows, puddling
the space between us.

In this day room
I must peel away the scaly layers
of your casing to unearth
some remnants of your life,
the blessing of little things
gifting themselves to memory,
carving their shapes in my mouth
like a river's erosion.

And this I know –
everything you gave to me remains.
For even as the particles of sand
sift through their hourglass,
no grain is ever lost,

and I will see you as you were,
your tortoise shell shouldering me
and shouldering me still.

GOING UNDER

I should have known when we met
that you were out of your comfort zone,
set adrift from the familiar to flounder
in the flotsam of a callous sea
that was the place I took you to you didn't know.

'Coffee?' I asked,
and when I joined the queue to pay
I watched you check your bag –
and check your bag a dozen times again
before your eyes hurried to search me out.

I loved you in that pause between our knowing –
you mother, in me, and I in you,
while somewhere near I heard the opening
and closing of a till and saw you reach
to check your bag and check again your bag,

seeking comfort in the familiar flotsam
of your life, while I could only watch you drowning
in that place I took you to you didn't know.

LEACHED

Your watered eyes seep
the recognition of the lost,
as a ward's hum skulks
in every orifice and tube
and every breath and suck
settling on the sizzling
spittle of your mouth.

I know its silent chant –
your wish to die,
If the Lord was good.
If the Lord was only good.

So I place my fingertips upon
the needle-bruising of your wrist
to sense beneath its surface a begrudging
acquiescence of the heart,
and let you go.

REQUIEM FOR THE UNBELIEVER

I lost my faith one dog-damp afternoon
in our mother's sitting room,
where her two-bar electric fire
sizzled heat in the unfamiliar space of her leaving.
On the sofa sat a man of religion taking notes,
scratching empathy onto the blank pages
of our mother's life, his sacred scribblings
setting out an order of service for her funeral.
Psalm twenty-three; a reading from Corinthians 13;
two favoured hymns; his own address
about a life well-lived and dutiful to God.
But the poem she had loved so much, denied.

She had found it in a book she'd read,
when words had sculpted shapes,
like breath, around the contours of her mouth,
their meanings sentient as any holy water tears.
Listen to my footfall in your heart, it said,
I am not gone but merely walk within you –
a message redolent of all those Sunday sermons
steeped in Christian kindliness and understanding.
Yet in that sitting room, it would not do
to set a precedent, for even the departed faithful
had to learn to play the rules. And so, I acquiesced
and left the room, my apostasy finally complete.

WHY YOU SHOULD ALWAYS LISTEN TO YOUR MOTHER

When my daughter got her ears pierced
she crumpled to the tiles like a sudden
exhalation of some ancient accordion.
She had done everything properly.
Respectable salon, clean equipment,
staff practised in the art of gun control.
I suppose it was the shock,
followed later by septic lobes
that no amount of boiled and
salted water could eradicate.

I remembered once, a student house,
kettle on the boil, a sewing needle
sterilised between each perforation.
Five of us and me the last to go,
ice cube sandwiched earlobes,
numb and dripping, as I waited for my turn
and prayed that by the time she came to me,
my housemate's pinhole accuracy had been sustained.
But I never had a minute's trouble,
earlobes both in perfect symmetry ever since.

PIANO LESSONS

This small room, its bay window hunched
from long years of partiality
to traffic noise outside – my sibling sits at a piano.

Hers are the hands I covet, those fingers
air-kissing the keys, that finely knuckled bridge
so effortlessly poised to play.

She goes first, being older and better to please
our teacher before the stumpy hammerings
of my own octaveless stretch.

Always on the table, while I wait,
an encyclopaedia, innards long succumbed
to seepages of wayward scales and dubious melodies.

I know the page, monochrome, edges sepia-singed with age
and here they are – ribbon, forked, staccato, bead, sheet –
imageries of sizzling electricity,

better than any piano lessons
or teachings in the rooms of my growing up.
Wonders unforced – lightning strikes to my reluctant tutelage.

JUMPS

No steeds were ever loved so much
as those we cosseted inside our heads –
our own two-legged beasts
galloping the garden of childhood,
willow wand whips in hand,
our fingers light on some imaginary rein.

We stole our histories from magazines,
named ourselves from aristocracy,
then fondly scissored neat rosettes
from tissue paper after school
and set a course cross-country
on our council house 'Estate'.

Two sisters, flying the jumps
of horse-backed summer afternoons,
where cut-out pictures on a bedroom wall
became your palomino and my russet bay,
the stamp of booted hooves upon a backdoor step,
the promise of a winded mane or red rosette.

JEFFERS

Two things I remember about Jeffers shop on High Street –
an unlocked cabinet of plastic animals and a citizen's arrest.
But first, the plastic animals, incarcerated in a place
where sibling breaths misted the polished glass
and podgy fingers poked their urgent imprint of intent.

Every Friday (pocket-money day), our mother walked us
through the council house estate, my older sister's
shiny half-a-crown forever blistering an expectant hole
into her palm, while in the pocket of my pinafore,
amongst the fray and fluff of childhood promises,
my lesser florin waited sulking and usurped.
Rules were tight, and woe betide a squabble for ownership
or our farmstead would endure an understock
for one more week.
So, we took our time, eying up those glassy pastures
like the seasoned ranchers that we were,
until our four and sixpence
worth of plastic homesteading was spent.

And then, one day, the citizen's arrest, which wasn't really
an arrest but more a lesson in morality,
curdling like that morning's breakfast whipped-up egg
within the marrow of my childhood bones.
The culprit was a boy I knew and the citizen his father,
shopping his son for something he had filched
the day before and stolen home. Humiliation in plain sight,
sweating its shame towards the crime I had earlier
scrunched into the smallness of my fist and that
I prayed would magically vanish unobserved
into the obscurity of a gutter, on our journey home.

THE SHORTS

At the bottom of our hill,
where a new road divided their house
from the rest of the world,
lived the Shorts. Mr and Mrs,
although I only ever spied him
the once – a galumph of his
one legged limp cautioning an enduring
suspicion in my eight-year-old self.

Our mother would send us down
with peelings in a bucket –
potatoes, carrots, onion skins
or anything else that Mrs Short's
menagerie of hungry fowl
could stomach after pulverisation
in some mysterious receptacle
grumbling in an outlawed lean-to.

Once, my brother snuck me in there
with a secret – unthinkable
scenes of slaughter already whetting
my imagination like a bad spell.
But the place was a soft harbour
of dusk light and warmth,
and from a corner, the blind mewing
of newborns nippling their mother's roundness.

Days later, I would check to find the imprints
of their little bodies on a drench of straw,
a pail of water close, the cat long vanished,
and me a bucketful of questions never clarified.
All part of growing up, but when a few years on
that clearance truck drove past our house,

I saw amongst the leftovers of someone's life,
a wooden leg,
and couldn't help but feel myself avenged.

WHAT REMAINS

'Please will you come and see my war crime?'

Of everything
this is what finally broke me –
the request small, polite.

A father.
The body of his dead boy
in a coffin car of cold and bloody dark.

This one old man.
This son.
This love.

SING

From a gape-mouthed sky
the ash clouds of your dead

shed their bruising like skin,
and below, a city chokes

upon the scurf of war,
waiting even for the bees

to sing again
the beauty of your name,

Mariupol.

My First Knee

A coil of concertina wire
serpenting bone-dried space,
red shirt and grey pants
speaking nothing of age,
parameters down
to how he holds a stone.
Minor or adult, sometimes hard
to tell the difference.

Everything I trained for
distils to this,
breath stilled, gaze unturned,
while a sniper's law cradles
within my curved finger.
But the Ruger is kind,
it will incapacitate,
a Barak would just detach his leg.

I will keep the casings,
even those 'two for one' errors
when a bullet carries through.
So, I ask for authorisation –
one more hit.
We're only talking knees.
Clearly, we shouldn't
liquidate the kids.

Winding Sheet

There you are,
wrapped inside the bindings of war,
only the short length of you to guess your age.
And there, your mother waits,
a stillness of grief
before the unravelling.

No flag tells us your story,
only the merge of white on red,
as layer after layer after layer
the bandages unpick,
and through an opening,
only big enough to place
a mother's goodbye kiss,
that glimpse of who you were.

So, there you are,
wrapped inside the bindings of war,
now disappeared along a corridor
of television news.
Some things you can't unsee
in the unwrapping. Nor ever should.

UNKNOWN 99

There is a baby
in the hospital labelled
Unknown 99
like some odd, uninteresting gift
relegated to the nameless list,

but I will call you
Little Miracle
and dare to think about
the who it is
you might become

when time transports you
to a place of
cradling light,
where displaced names
have lost their anonymity,

where the moon can chase
the stars in limpid skies,
and where silence sheds
its longing into sleep
like melted snow.

I see you there,
war's *Little Miracle*,
your belly full again,
your heart the beating presence
of a nation's grief.

PIGEON FOOD

This morning, in the soft beauty
of my garden, I fed seed to the birds.
Pheasants, blue tits, robins
and a single woodpecker,
some long-tailed tits, a murderhood of crows,
two magpies and a jackdaw chick.
But no pigeons.

Later, on the television news,
and in that place
where birdsong's
scorched mouth drones
the skies in open stealth,
I find where all those hungry
disappeared have flown.

A peoplehood of humankind,
and last among the pecking-order list,
they are being offered pigeon food for breakfast.

GÖTTERDÄMMERUNG*

When you say that you just can't look

Look
and rinse your eyes
with hearts that
fall and rise and fall
until Allah finally admits
their stillness into martyrdom

Look
and see how suffering
fails to penetrate the consciousness
of a world where the umbilici
are severed with stones
and limbs dispensed with Gigli saws

Look
and know that weed fields
never feed the starved
nor a coverall of PPE dispel
the clenching teeth of children's misery
and that all roads lead to death

Look
and wonder that enough
just never seems to be enough
and when we turn away
we become complicit
by our own abstentions.
Look

* *Götterdämmerung: Situations of world altering destruction marked by
extreme chaos and violence*

33

RIGHT OF RETURN

In the dustbowl of his palm, a key.

He knows its searing
coolness on his skin,
its metal imprint sewn
like a tattoo into the fabric
of his dreams, while
the parched mouth of a lock
screams in a door
somewhere in the past,
waiting for a homecoming,

waiting for a miracle.

HARDCORE

Children lick plastic bags like lollipops,
tongues stretched into corners,
tastebuds alert for the tang
of a honeyed moon
while trucks carry cargo to the sea,
a stew of rubble and bones,
and foundation for a too-late promise
built upon the splintered remains
of the disappeared.

UNBROKEN

You may think you have silenced us,
but the voices of our forefathers
still sing along the sheared streets
of your destruction.

You may think you have orphaned us,
but every soul owns its paradise
and every loss still breathes
in those who are left behind.

You may think you have famished us,
but our stripped bones will one day
permeate the soil, nurturing the promise
of new beginnings.

You may think you have demolished us,
but even the crush of what remains
can learn to be again its own foundation
and a country reborn.

You may think you have buried us,
but we will ghost your consciousness
in the small hours of your sleeping,
haunting all of your imaginings.

You may think you have broken us,
but we are stronger than you know.
Stronger because of you.
Stronger, despite you.

WHAT IS WRONG WITH YOU?

When you sleep, do you think of them in your dreams?
I do wonder about that. And I think it must be easier
to partner the devil than to sift through lies
that burn and scald and break the rest of us.

I pity you.

For while the rising souls of Gazan dead
find peace in martyrdom, you will face the sentence
of your own deliverer; past deeds forever rotting
in an unforgiving coffin of your inhumanity.

THIS DECENT LIFE

My pheasants have a life,
a decent life,
their thirsts satisfied
with a single swallow,
their hunger soothed
by offerings of easy kindliness.
Easy kindliness, and the knowing
that decency does not always afford
safe passage, even for a simple bird.

Her shredded body lay on the field,
a spill of fresh silage
sprinkled over her like buckshot –
a foot missing, innards laid bare
by the cut of the blades
and a freckling of feathers
peeled from their pink bones –
still warm as she was lifted.

I buried the pieces of her
in a place her friends might know,
her lost presence new to them
in the aftermath. A decent burial.
But what to say about so small a thing,
these words about a bird and not a bird
no solace to the left behind,
no succour to the suffering,
no answer to the never-ending pain of war.

AFTERTHOUGHT

Tell the displaced they will find a home,
if they do not die while walking.

Tell the maimed that in five years' time
they will have learned to crawl again.

Tell the buried they will only live
inside the beating hearts of those remaining.

Tell the orphaned that the sympathy of others
will never heal their loneliness.

Tell the abandoned they may one day
be remembered for their fortitude.

Tell the starved that *skin and bone*
has satisfied its own hyperbole.

Tell the missing they are simply numbers now,
lost within the ether of statistics and conveniency.

Tell the children you have not forgotten them
when their images have ceased to occupy our TV screens.

Tell whoever wants to listen that the world is surely lost
if the dead are but an afterthought.

WANT

A silence of drones finds solace
in an empty sky,
and below,
hope.

I Should have Brought you Home

You never asked, and nor did I;
the waiting crisis of your broken hip
putting those decisions on a kind of hold
as words stayed stifled in the silence
of our muted throats.

Yet now it's far too late
to do things differently
and own that change of circumstance
of me become the mother, you, the child,
with nurture somewhere in between.

How easily then does history reveal itself
in ways we choose to snub;
looking back the easy and the hardest part
of what we could or should have done,
or what we did.

So, know that if I had the chance
to do it all again
I would have loved you
more than just enough,
and brought you home.

AND SO IT IS

My chest is numb,
the meaty breast of it
as plump and pink
as supermarket turkey thighs,
the scanner's machine breath
a soft whirr of sound
like the inside of a prayer.

Three good samples
or we go again.

A needle probes
between the boned fence
of my ribs, its journey
to the lining of the lung
savouring its own spotlight
on a computer screen
next door.

In the search for stillness
I swallow time.

Pressure meets itself
inside the casing of my chest,
a fly fisher's precision
finding its mark
where every sample counts
and every mystery unfurls
its secret.

Cautious hands pleat upon
the ticking clock of my chest.

Then at the last,
that rising fizz of blood
behind my throat –
the quid pro quo
of services exchanged,
reminder that even prayer will
ultimately consign itself to fate.

So now,
we wait.

EVACUATIONS

I wish I could write about the scorched tongue of your
suffering and how it shrivels in the heat of a thousand suns
and a thousand guns on an airport road.

I wish I could write about the parched soul of your despair
and how the sapling limbs of children stretch towards
an abandonment of light.

I wish I could write about the terror that wracked your
sleeps, where, in hidden rooms, shrapnel scabs its graffiti
like a shroud on secret walls.

I wish I could write about you with words crafted in hope,
chiselling meaning into the granite cavalcade
of promises, long made of dust.

I wish I could write that Jannah waits for you in foreign
soil, where the home you carry finds a kind of healing
in the benevolence of strangers.

And I wish that you will meet the shame of our betrayal
with a generous and forgiving heart.
Man ârezoo mikonam. I wish.

THE LETTING
Auschwitz/Birkenau

There remains yet the odour of absence
and a silent keening of ghosts
that suppurates in weeping walls.
On stoned pathways the hushed footfall
of the dead still treads its beat,
marking time for souls selected
for their usefulness,
a finger's point away from
one more beating heart or none.

In concrete corridors
the brittle-eyed speak now
from simple frames – their history,
a name, the date arrived and date deceased
(a day, a month, but rarely more between)
while unframed faces suffer still in anonymity,
their ashes fertilized efficiently
(no wastage here), the debris of those lives
now earthed beneath a sea
of fast fermented tears.

I cannot think too much of it,
for I am chased by thoughts
of things I did not know nor want to know.
For the odour of absence
seeps its disregarded souvenirs
into our selective memory, while history
sleeps on in other ghosted walls,
or hidden corners where is found the letting still.

THE LEAVING

She left for school pretty in gingham
the heels of her socks halfway up
the back of skinny legs

a ponytail's auburn sway
waving its flippant farewell
at a mother's angst

leaving day
the first and only time
I let her walk to school

alone

later I took a tear from the corner
of her eye where it waited
like a water droplet caught upon a leaf

surprised

'Killed in Crossfire'
a twenty second soundbite
on the local news

yet every second marked a year of absence
when a tissue waited in a drawer
and one dried tear remained the only thing I had

but even that has
evaporated now
to nothingness

WHEN THE RAINS FAILED

When the rains failed nothing grew,
and wasted seeds dimpled dry earth
like buckshot. Yet words still spoke
behind the shroud of her eyes –
words that painted promises;
sorghum, baobab, cassava, akkerboon –
she ensured the children's tongues
would never snag in their telling.

On schoolless days their books were crops
that shelved themselves in dusty drills
and twigs could pencil rows of seedlings,
one by one. Learning seeped through soil
like water earned, an education underfoot
from home to well and back again –
a daughter's quest for knowledge,
a son's unearthing of himself.

Here she stands; nurturer, protector, guide,
mothering the present and holding her ground.
For this would be their harvest of hope,
its lexicon of meaning written into earth
where tiny miracles stretch
towards the sun, their blossoming gifts
a storybook of promises, made good
through languages of love.

PATHFINDERS

The starlings are back,
making voices in the eaves,
scuttling noisily
through the residue
of last year's debris,
keeping me awake.
The past welcomes them
with familiarity, nothing more,
and through spring and summer
nature will absorb the sludge
from their wintered bones.
I lie in bed, imagining soon
the scaldies, clutching, like bees,
to the others' legs in sleep,
dreaming of the pilgrimage
of flights to come.

I think of all those journeys
now unfulfilled,
and absences
that scuff like spindrift
on the surfaces of seas,
or hearts left sundered
from the haemorrhage
of human touch.
Yet as the world's
dark shadows cede,
like fledglings
we will know the tug
of a forgiving sky,
where dreams have wings
and every pilgrimage
a hope fulfilled.

The Sadness of Crows

Before the day opens its eyes,
on a fence
two black crows,
their thistle throats
rinsing the morning
with sorrow.

If I could
I would offer them
the fragile bones
of a vanished chick,
its soul seeping quietly
into warm-dug earth.

I would tell them
it lay now in softest tissue,
belly feathers fluffed
and eyes of lazuline
puzzling the injustices
of 'going light'.

For in the night
my sleep had met
their fledgless child
and I had known the flutter
of its death kiss
on my cheek.

Later, the boneyard
of my garden
would fold its limbs
about that curl of wing
and clutch of claw
in final flight.

Before the day closes its eyes,
on a fence, two crows,
messaging the sky
with longing for
a small remaining breath
in a dying afternoon.

A Mouse's Tale

Autumn exhales,
her heavy breath sucked
into the lungs of a coming winter,
while the garden shivers.

Leaves, mulched
by frost and weeping skies,
settle into corners,
nuisancing themselves
in drains all around the house.

Spent stems spike from
wrinkling soil, the wilted summer
blooms surrendered long ago,
their thirsts depleted,
and from the pharynx of an ancient
watering can, a string.

The spongy wet slime of it
droops like ice-melt on the rim,
and when I tug,
from my fingers
drools a mouse's tail,
its remainder entombed within
the death spout of impossible escape.

I shake the bloated corpse
from its confinement,
see, within the watery belly of the can,
that long, exaggerated death
and a purgatory of neither
future nor of past. No lesson here,
only the remnants of life cut short
by the cruel randomness of fate.

SHOOTING PARTY

Sunshine shirks the day
and out in the thickening light
their conversation visits me
like a clattering of plates.
These birds, a nye of ambered beauty,
strut my lawn with a conspiracy of dames –
I know them by heart and will let their chatter
carry into fearless sleep; time yet
to fear for their feathered lives.

Tomorrow will come the hunters
in their tweeds and their conceit,
peppering buckshot over my roof like bloodied ash
as a posh nosh van flies up the lane
and beaters beat death into twenty feet of sky.
What do those brave men say when they go home?
'Such a great day's sport –
I slaughtered ten or more, but never mind,
the dogs' soft mouths were eager to retrieve.'

HEDGE AND HARROW

Hogged mane on a drumlin's back,
rolling stubby and stout
on far and lonely fields
where once a horse and man
combined to follow the contours
of your spiny neck.

The sound of lift and fold
on furrow of claddy earth,
as plough and beast
unite in slog and sweat
till dusk is set
and a day's work finally complete.

AFTER

They are still out there,
the birds – singing.

Can you hear?

The world is alive,
throating its resilience

with nature's tomorrow songs.

THERE ARE LISTS AND THERE ARE LISTS

Eighty-six chickens
Fifty-six dogs (one in labour)
Ten rabbits
Four parakeets
Three cats
Eight snakes
One pheasant
Five hundred and thirty-one
mice, rats and hamsters
One gecko
Three sugar sliders
One hundred and twenty-seven
marijuana plants
Seventeen guns

One child

What It Does to You

The intrigue
the plain brown envelope
the name misspelt
the address carelessly penned
with ambivalence
by an unknown hand

Interesting

The opening
the folded white A4
the photocopied sheet
(no prints but mine then)
the three-line of loathing
magnified in black ink

Really?

The follow up
the police, the questions
the who why what when
of the perpetrator
the forensics
the threat

For fuck's sake

The aftermath
the wondering
the knowing that life
has altered just like that
the boiling anger at the risk
you suddenly need to take

just to put your name upon a bloody poem

ANTE MORTEM

Along a death road
from post to post
the corbies sleep;
their shit-stained shadows
flumped from flaccid wings,
leaching the stagnant earth
as the world grieves – testa
pecked away to haemorrhage
the human pus within;
this last evisceration
to the cleansing of itself.
For what we were
we have again become,
primordial in conceit;
our bodies snagged between
the living or the dead,
our souls exposed and seeping
as the corbies in their sleep
begin to stir.

COUP DE GRACE

I tether myself to a moment
when the past slides
to freckled shade
and the day finds sleep,
chiselling a feather's worth
of words from the present.

In this place skies remain
unpunctured with the memory
of what will be or what was,
and I must be thankful
for the beauty of the now.

But I am searching for that place
where birds go when they die –
when flight has stilled and
fragile bones sponge into earth.

A place where finally
all searching feels complete
and beauty is forever swallowed whole
into an absence of anything that was.

FE 2O3

From skinned and tendered ribs
detritus sleeches, soft tissue lost
beneath a century of salted tears.

Only the galvanised survives,
she feels its tingle on her tarnished hull,
an acid tongue that licks through
every orifice and naked bone
or seeps from rusticles like
poisoned pus of weighted time.

Yet on she sleeps companioned
by the ghosted souls who wait,
like her, condemned to history now,

the drowning ship of dreams.

INCEPTION

Earth's tautness tingles like an acned curse,
the empty stomach of her hunger
rumbling on ocean tides, lapping tears
on sterile shores.

She mourns her rugose beauty,
the contoured history that moulded her
filched by the botoxed plumpness
of a promised immortality.

For this is the new world, a death-wish world,
wallowing in the pleasures of its own destruction
and flattering itself with the poisons
of an acid reflux kiss.

But underneath the surface of her skin
and far below that barborygmus core,
earth awaits the stirring
of a sleeping seed.

For the end finds a beginning
in its final breath, when all that is left,
all that is left, is the vagitus
of a waiting world unborn.

SKUNKED

The Cowboy Mall
Stillwater, Oklahoma
Summer 1982

I am serving tables in The House of Greek.
Outside on the street
air stifles with a promise
while a tornado bides its time
across the Sooner Plains
and sirens smirk
on waiting intersections.
I take a smoke break,
watch the shoppers tramp
a central thoroughfare until
their Lowry-esque mutations
fossilize into the nostril twitching
canvas of the mall.
A skunk is trapped between
two entrance doors,
its leached mephitis perforating
orifice and pore as easily as smoke
and shoppers wane like ghosts
behind the slap of shop store shutters.
Yet I have smelt much worse back home
where cordite chewed an endless souvenir
through flesh and bone and blood
to leave its permanence tattooed
upon the skin.
No different then
this trespasser and I,
both stalked within our casings
and forever shackled
by the curse of our constraint
until we die.

FROM THIS NORTHERN WINDOW

I see your landscape through
the double-glazing of my Irishness:
mountain, river, lake and bog,
falling upon each other
in a slant of summer greens
and winter greys.

Yet I am torn in my belonging,
these northern eyes of mine
long trained to scan for that
which steals away our oneness,
shrivelling the view,
colour-washing earth and sky.

I search for ties that bind us
in our estranged vernaculars,
meeting their reflection
in the two-way glass
of an identity that transcends
my own unease.

But at the end I claim the Irish
of a common soil, where earth
does not secern between our differences
and meaning shares itself
unselfishly with only this –
the need to call you 'home'.

FOLDED

You are an envelope
unopened,
chin to chest,
face to thigh –
Li Hua,
the folded man,
twenty-eight years
in search of sky.

There is no easy
unfurling,
no gentle tease
of bony curves,
no tender touch,
no fond and soft
caress of tendons,
sinews, nerves.

Only the scraich
of saw on bone,
on thigh, on neck,
on lumbar spine
and finally on hips
to help you stand,
the folded man,
unfolded by design.

Your mother,
Tang Dongchen,
will see your face
and know it whole,
and sifting through
the stones of memory

say, my son,
I met your soul.

Unbound by love
the burden
of your folding
finds release
in eyes that
after all this time
will kiss the sky
to find you peace.

* *The 'Folded Man' was diagnosed with* ankylosing spondylitis *in 1991
at the young age of 18.*

DO NOT SPEAK TO ME OF SILENCE
i.m. Helen McCrory

It has been a week
since he held your voice,
its absence filtering
between that final curve
of breath and now.

He searches for its sustain
in the fragments
of you remaining,
shadowed in the sculpture
of his empty palms.

He will not know
this silence you have
tricked him with,
for even now
your voice conceals

itself in crevices
he has yet to find –
that cruel punchline,
waiting to catch him
unawares.

MARINELLA BERETTA

You, with the beautiful name,
slumped in your living room,
a ghosted parchment of yourself
mummified by air, by cold, by solitude.

Your hands still stretch on rotted chair-arms,
slender fingers anticipating flight
like some eager concert pianist
waiting for their grand finale.

Not four seasons, but eight,
visited before the finding of you;
a macabre story on the web
and shame for a community.

I wonder about you –
your loneliness at the end
or the beginning and how it was
your heart was finally stilled.

Your unknown face is my imagining now,
the tissued softness of your skin
as lucent as the light that burned a fire
behind the amber of your eyes.

And in this sorrow there remains
that part of you still scorched through time –
your name; its beauty weaved into the pattern
of a life you left behind.

QUIET HOUSES

Choked with the dregs of your leaving,
these evening hours trail their tired feet
towards the sleep of my hollow company,
where a bed's too big and the space remaining
clings cool as metal to my bare skin.

I think of those other quiet houses;
the creak of stairs conversation enough
for lonely souls to feed upon,
or a vixen's tortured cry
offering solace across wintering fields.

And here, within my solitary walls,
an absence now conceals itself
in corners like a shadow's breath,
its reluctant presence forever doused
within the cavities of these aching bones.

CODA

Fingertips stroke their melody over piano keys
as easily as a river's heartbeat finds its home
upon the silted beds of summer, every note
a serenade across the stage, aching into
crevices and spilling stories redolent
of what was or what could impossibly be.
Her feathered touch would tempt an audience
to breathe those cadences of pitch and tone,
the music's waiting surprise concealed within
an abrupt suspension of her hands.

Captured then, the tacet of her disbelief,
when notes became an unpredicted
wall of silence on the stave, and all of life
has altered in that single metronomic beat.
No grand accelerando to foretell her fate,
only the bewildered hush of onlookers
scalded by a shock of words left hanging
like some caesura noose in hollowed space.

      'I don't know where I am.'
      'I don't know where I am.'

DANCER

Wearied she seems,
stooped, like barley beard,
forlorn and wetted
after summer rain.

Her back now arched
with memory of long ago,
when she was full of elegance
from tip to toe,

her dancing feet
then poised to fly
across the dusty boards,
but that was long and long ago.

Wearied now, she is
(though lovely still)
she stands upon the shore
and picks a shoe –

a dancing shoe
from off the pebbles underfoot.
A sad and lonely thing
it has become,

abandoned where the water laps
and licks her naked toes.
What good one shoe
for anyone to keep she thinks,

yet picks it up,
to softly store away
the memory of dusty boards
and whispers of her dancing feet.

HOW SHE LEFT THE HOUSE

It was as she left it, unknowing of her absent return,
everything ached in neatness because
for such a while there had been only her.
She went out to buy milk or walk in the fields
or take a drive or meet a secret love
or catch a breather from her inside world.
It did not matter why. For dead is always
going to be dead and everything remaining,
ever unexplained.

They would wonder at the question marks
now hanked for the unravelling
in lonesome rooms. Those leavings
soon to be dismantled or misunderstood –
an indistinct initial on a calendar perhaps,
a half-aired bed, the clatter of a thousand
bits and pieces of her precious ordinary life,
ghosted in the shadows of an empty house
she never meant to leave behind.

YOU

You have borne the weight of war
upon your brittle bones
and shouldered its burden
until your buckling knees
wheezed like cancered lungs.

You have rested beneath
a sterility of trees
whose naked fingers
clawed the sky above for breath,
finding only contaminated air.

You have carried your pain
to that place of enough,
where hidden in its crevices
you find the famished
seeds of what could be.

You have arrived
at a shore of beginnings,
though the weight of waves
can still smother, and sand
still scorch your feet.

You have stripped bare
the starkness of who you are,
offering up your trust
to the kindness of others
like a heart exposed.

You have learned that love
is more than just a solitary word
but a path to belonging
that weaves through the story
of you and finally finds a home.

REPAIR
for my homeland

Years have ghosted their quarter century into the past,
our brokenness healed only by an impatient future
pleading to us through the voices of our children.

Time still aches with losses hard to set aside,
its great yawn of shadows stretched behind us
in an unforgiving dark that stutters the way ahead.

Yet I will take your seven hundred days of failure
for a single one of hope, when the imperfections of our past
can melt into the cracks of our repair like a kintsugi kiss.

Then, from the fragments of our differences will grow
a kind of beauty of its own, bound fast by faith and trust,
and finally blessed with the promise of a lasting peace.

SMART

There's this tiny Smart car
parked outside our building,
its flat front tyre pressing
a smushy kiss into the concrete.

There's a *please help me*
finger-scrawled across
the milky windows of desert dust,
ruining their sight.

And there's a key in the ignition,
waiting for a car hire firm
to track its abandonment
and hobble it back home.

WHAT THE HEART KNOWS

Across the lake
a wedge of swans
flies by instinct
in arrowed flight,
their wingbeat thrum
a unison of breaths
as intimate as love itself.

I watch them vanish
into chartless skies,
the transience of their beauty
now become a riffle
in memory that
pulses in the chambers
of my heart.

But beyond what we see
the heart remembers –
a full-leafed summer
the colour of possibilities
and winter's bareness
kissed with the promise
of a coming spring.

And the kindnesses we share
will wait to meet us
on that other side,
as the unknown offers up
its borrowed light
and finds a home again
in all our chartless skies.

BETWEEN TWO HEARTS

The distance between two hearts
is measured not in words of creed,
where God and Allah
vie to take the upper hand.

Nor is it measured by a debt of culture
when the rhythms of its beat
are swallowed up by ritual
and obligation.

The distance between two hearts
is measured always in our love,
where every bridge we cross
becomes a treasured memory
of what we gave and gained
together through our lives.

And if we listen closely
we will hear its echo
touch another's heart,
as you touched mine

and always let me soar.

BREAST TALK

Strange
how we can speak
so easily of breasts.

When he supplanted
one of mine
the surgeon's eyes
were gloating satisfaction
at its matching symmetry.

Yet I could only see
that baby's suck,
so slightly left of centre
and a puckered souvenir
of what was lost.

So strange, it is,
how easily
we speak of breasts.

In Omnia Paratus

This is how it used to be,
the unknown still a gift,
its treasures taste-touched
upon our waiting tongues.
The sky was then
a spill of cerulean blue
and the promise of us
ignited me like a spark.

Odd for me to think of it
with everything that's
happened in between.
How life can shrug its
shoulders at the past
knowing that what matters now
is how you'd always jump for me
and me for you.

CENTERED

A dampness of sheets
bandages my eight-year-old legs,

their seeped coldness assaulting
these young bones like claws of frost

on an inside windowpane.
Parlour voices blur cadences

through a thin dividing wall,
as I wait, wait, for my sister's spooning warmth

that shield from outside darkness,
where silence sifts away

some howling dog across the bog
to finally send me into sleep.

AT THE LAST

It was in the knowing,
friendship brimming the years
with not so much a last goodbye
but an adventure into something else.

You before me, showing the way.

It was in the knowing,
finding you later
in the little things that
no one else would care about.

The hole that is filled with what you left.

It was in the knowing,
our understanding
of your leaving never
breached by sadnesses.

For as the heart sings it leaves its melody behind.

It was in the knowing,
laughter settling still
upon the waiting shelves
of strangers as it falls.

And at the last, the knowing of the other's love.

ENDINGS

Death meets us all,
spilling its shadow
into the unknown;
the curve of our lives
completing itself in endings
frayed by private histories.

And those we leave behind
will know their grief the same;
the privileged, the ordinary,
whose sorrow sings on different winds,
yet every song a sharing
of its own ineffable loss.

What would be my life's story?

To have been loved,
warts and all.

It's enough.

ACKNOWLEDGEMENTS

Thanks to the editors of the following in which some of these poems appeared: *Lothlorien Poetry Journal, Live Encounters, Abridged, Skylight47, Central Bylines, Drawn to the Light, Eat the Storm, Bangor Literary Journal, Dreich magazine, The Galway Review, CAP Seamus Heaney Anthology, Atunis Galaxy, Ablucionistas Journal, Shop Irish Writers,* The Irish Centre for Poetry Studies, Fiery Arrows Press.

'Pouffe' was shortlisted for *The Bangor Literary Journal* Poetry Competition 2024.

'A Village Practice' was highly commended for The Westival International Poetry Competition 2023.

'Piano Lessons' was highly commended for The King Lear Prize 2021.

'Day Room Days' was longlisted for The Trim Poetry Competition 2023.

'Cold Tea' was placed third in The Westival International Poetry Competition 2020 while 'The Sadness of Crows' was highly commended.

Sincere thanks and appreciation to my family and friends for the support they have given me with my writing over the years. Special regards to Eileen Casey, my stalwart, mentor and friend who has always guided me with her gentle words of encouragement and advice; to Robyn Rowland, always an inspiration since the day of our first meeting. I am very grateful, once again, to Alan Hayes of Arlen House for his continued support of my poetry, and to the Arts Council of Northern Ireland, without whom collections like mine would surely struggle to come to fruition. I owe a huge debt to the members of my writing class who have supported me faithfully through the rough and the smooth – your friendship and camaraderie have kept me going more that you can possibly know. Finally, enormous gratitude to Emma Barone whose artwork is truly a thing of beauty. I am so thankful for the privilege of using the wonderful image 'Blackbird Incognito' as the cover for this, my second poetry collection.

Lynda Tavakoli spent many years abroad before returning home to her native Northern Ireland where she worked as a special needs teacher and creative writing facilitator. Her prose and poetry have been published in Ireland and internationally, both in print and online. Her debut collection of poetry, *The Boiling Point for Jam* (Arlen House, 2020) was internationally acclaimed. She is included in The Index of Contemporary Writers in Ireland and is a professional member of the Irish Writers Centre.

She has won poetry and short story prizes in Listowel, the Westival International Poetry Prize, the Mencap International Short Story Prize, and was runner-up in the Blackwater and Roscommon poetry competitions. She has been nominated for the Pushcart Prize 2024 and Best of the Net Awards 2024/2025. Some of her work has been translated into Farsi and Spanish.

Tavakoli is also the author of two novels *Of Broken Things* and *Attachment,* and a short story anthology *Under a Cold White Moon* (David James Publishing). Most recently she published her first digital e-book about dementia, *The Greying Wood of Trees* (Live Encounters 2024).